Charlie's JOURNEY

Shannon Kelly Dass

AuthorHouse™
1663 Liberty Drive
Bloomington, IN 47403
www.authorhouse.com
Phone: 833-262-8899

This book is printed on acid-free paper.

ISBN: 978-1-6655-1541-2 (sc)
ISBN: 978-1-6655-1539-9 (hc)
ISBN: 978-1-6655-1540-5 (e)

Print information available on the last page.

Published by AuthorHouse 01/27/2021

authorHOUSE®

To two of the most beautiful people I know, my mom and dad, who have always believed in my writing.

To my students, who teach me every single day.

Beep, beep, beep.

I blink several times and suddenly remember it's the first day of school! I jump up, stretch my arms into the air, and let out a big yawn. I have a big smile as the first day of school excitement begins to take over.

"Charlie, come down for breakfast!" Mom is making her first day of school specialty; the smell of French toast lingers in the air. I slip my head through my first day of school T-shirt and step into my first day of school shorts.

"Charlie, slow down! You're going to make yourself sick," Mom exclaims as I shovel in my French toast soaked with maple syrup and topped with powdered sugar.

"I'm done! Let's go!" I slide my arms through the straps of my backpack and slip on my sneakers.

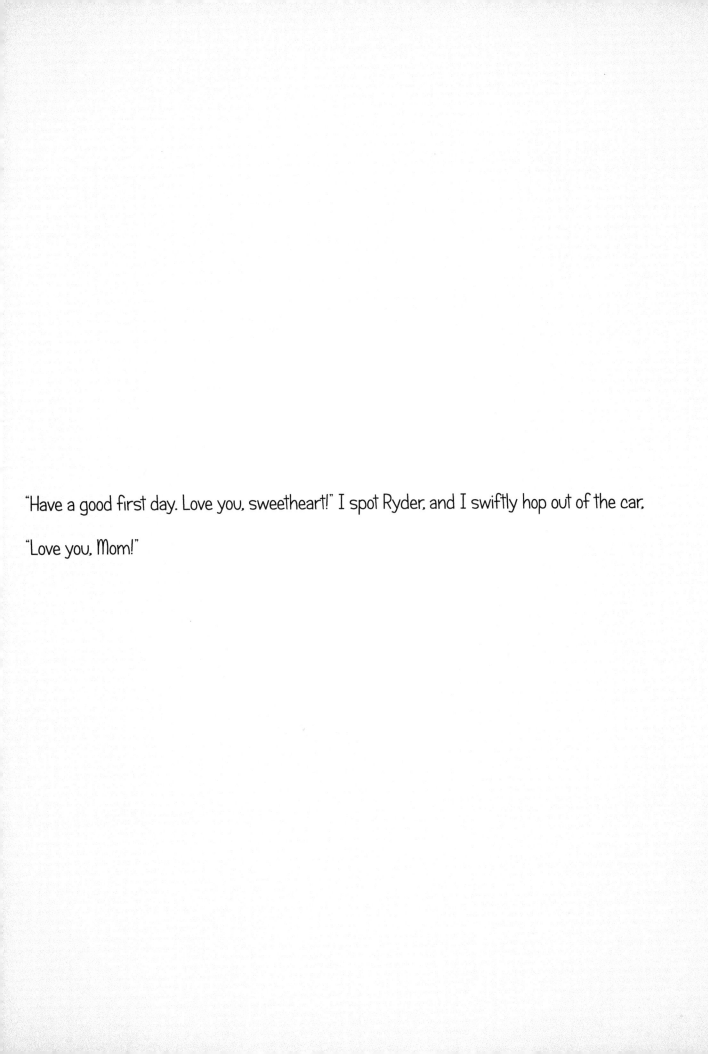

"Have a good first day. Love you, sweetheart!" I spot Ryder, and I swiftly hop out of the car.

"Love you, Mom!"

The bell rings, and it's time to head inside. I walk with Ryder as we try to find the door marked, "Ms. Davis."

"Hurry up! It's over here." Ryder found the door already; he's such a quick reader. I jog up to him, and we enter the room.

"Good morning, third graders! Please find your desks. Your names are printed at the top." Ms. Davis has a nice smile.

All right, Charlie, look for Charlie.

I peer over, and Ryder is sitting at his desk.

How is he always such a fast reader? I wonder.

I read the name on the first desk. "Miles." That's not me. I read the name on the next desk. "Ja, Jack? Oh, Jake!" That's not me. I glance around and realize almost everyone has found their desks.

That's strange. They must all be really quick readers, like Ryder.

"Charlie, you are over here." I look up at Ms. Davis's gentle smile. She leads me to my desk.

"One, two, three, eyes on me," Ms. Davis calls.

"One, two, eyes on you," we repeat.

"Well done, everyone! All right, friends, we are entering free time! Please keep the noise level at a 4."

Ryder and I move quickly over to the computers and log on to the program 1, 2, 3, Math. "Let's see who can complete the questions quicker!" Ryder exclaims.

"Sure!" I already know Ryder is going to win. He always wins at this game.

"Charlie?" I turn to see Ms. Davis standing behind us.

"Yeah?" I respond.

"Charlie, please log off the computer. I have someone I want you to meet." I shrug at Ryder and log off the computer, just as Ms. Davis asked. I walk over to her desk. She is standing with someone I haven't seen before.

"Charlie, this is Ms. Kennan," Ms. Davis explains.

"Hello, Charlie. It's nice to meet you," Ms. Kennan reaches her hand out to shake mine.

Ms. Davis explains that Ms. Kennan is the Resource Room teacher, and she's going to pull me out of class sometimes. She said that we are going to work on some reading and writing stuff. She said she might even come into class sometimes and work with me here.

I guess that's kind of cool. Ms. Kennan seems nice.

"Okay," I respond shyly.

Ring, ring, ring!

The sound of the bell tells us it's time to go home. Ryder and I tumble over each other as we race down the hall to see who can reach the front doors first.

"Slow down, boys! We don't want anyone to get hurt," Mr. Parker calls out. Mr. Parker is the commander of the halls. You want to be on his good side.

"Sorry, Mr. Parker!" We slow down until we are out of his sight. Then we giggle as we pick up speed again.

The sun warms my face as I spot Mom in the crowd.

"See you tomorrow," I say. I high-five Ryder and run toward Mom.

On the walk home, I tell Mom all about Ms. Kennan. Mom seems pleased. "That sounds like it will be really helpful for you, Charlie."

Mom's always right.

The next morning, as we are about to start language arts, Ms. Kennan walks into the room. She pulls a chair up next to me. "Hi, Charlie. I'm going to join you during language arts if that's okay with you."

"Sure." I smile.

Ms. Davis starts the lesson and keeps using the word, "theme". I'm not really sure what it means, but she sure is using it a lot. I look over at Ryder, and he's nodding along as Ms. Davis is speaking.

Why does he always seem to know what she's talking about?

My thoughts are interrupted as Ms. Kennan whispers in my ear, "Every story that we read has a theme. It's a message. You have to ask yourself what the author is trying to tell you."

Oh, a message? I know what a message is.

I nod back at her.

Hey, I'm nodding like Ryder!

I smile and look back at Ms. Davis. Every time she says something that confuses me, Ms. Kennan is right there to explain it. When it comes time to complete the worksheet, I barely even need Ms. Kennan, but she is there if I have any questions, which is pretty cool.

Ring, ring, ring!

Recess!

Ryder and I rush out to the field with the rest of the class.

"Hey, over here!" Ryder is holding up a soccer ball.

"Nice! You got the new one." I smile.

"Miles, Kinsley! Charlie and I are playing over here!" Ryder motions to a couple of our classmates, and they jog toward us. We split into teams—me and Ryder versus Miles and Kinsley.

"Let's go!" Ryder sets the ball down in the center of the field.

"Hey, Charlie, you sure you don't need Ms. Kennan out here? I don't know if you and Ryder will be able to win without her." Miles laughs.

"Hey, that's not cool, Miles. Let's just play," Ryder snaps back at him.

My shoulders slump. I look over at Miles, who's still smiling.

Ms. Kennan stinks.

"One, two, three, eyes on me," Ms. Davis calls.

"One, two, eyes on you," we answer.

"All right, friends, it's time to get into our reading groups," Ms. Davis announces.

I pull my book out of my desk. As I look up, I notice Ms. Kennan in the doorway. I sink low in my chair, hoping she won't see me. I gaze around the room to see if anyone else has noticed her yet, but everyone is too busy getting into their groups.

Ms. Davis walks toward me and whispers, "Go ahead, Charlie, Ms. Kennan is waiting for you. You'll work in her room for a little bit. Bring your book."

I get up slowly, hoping no one will notice me. Hanging my head, I drag my feet toward the door.

"What was the best part of your day?" Mom asks.

"There was no best part," I grumble.

"All right, why don't we start with the worst part of your day then?" Mom always knows when I've had a bad day.

"I don't want to work with Ms. Kennan anymore." I look away from Mom.

"Okay." Mom is quiet. I look at her, and she looks back at me. She smiles softly and runs her fingers through my hair. "Why don't you tell me what's really going on?"

"Miles ... Miles made fun of me during recess. He asked me if I needed Ms. Kennan to help me play soccer." Tears pool in my eyes, and I try to stop them from falling.

"Hmm, Miles. Well, do you need Ms. Kennan to help you play soccer?"

"No way! Ryder and I are unstoppable on the field." I can't help myself from giggling at the thought of Ms. Kennan on the field with us.

Mom smiles and pulls me into her, kissing me on the top of my head. "Sometimes other people, even our friends, don't always think about how their words could be hurtful. Now let me ask you something. When Ms. Kennan helps you, how does it make you feel?"

"Well it's like she always knows when I'm confused, and she gives me cool tips and tricks to remember things. So I guess when I'm working with her, it makes me feel kind of happy because I always know what's going on." I smile.

"She sounds awful. You must stop working with her immediately," Mom says sarcastically.

"Mom!" I laugh.

"One, two, three, eyes on me," Ms. Davis calls.

"One, two, eyes on you," we respond. The excitement of a Friday afternoon buzzes through the air.

"All right, friends, I am going to pass back your language arts quizzes. Please make sure you get them signed by your parents over the weekend," Ms. Davis says.

Ms. Davis walks toward me and places my quiz on my desk. My eyes grow wide. On my paper are a big gold star and 90 percent written in sparkly blue ink. I am mesmerized as I stare at the number.

Ninety percent!

Ring, ring, ring!

The end of the day bell startles me. I feel a hand on my shoulder.

"Charlie, come on!" I turn and see Ryder and Miles. They look down at the quiz in my hand.

"Hey, way to go, Charlie. Ninety percent!" Miles high-fives me. I can't help but smile.

"Thanks!"

"Race you guys outside!" Ryder takes off, and Miles and I follow suit. I make sure to hold on to my quiz extra tight though.

I can't wait to show Mom.

CPSIA information can be obtained
at www.ICGtesting.com
Printed in the USA
BVHW020838160221
600232BV00003B/6